Bear and Turtle

and the Great Lake Race

Andrew Fusek Peters

illustrated by
Alison Edgson

Child's Play (International) Ltd
Ashworth Rd, Bridgemead, Swindon, SN5 7YD UK
Swindon   Auburn ME   Sydney
Text © 2005 A. Fusek Peters   Illustrations © 2005 Child's Play (International) Ltd
ISBN 978-1-904550-91-4   CLP070711CPL0811914
Printed in Shenzhen, China
3 5 7 9 10 8 6 4 2
www.childs-play.com

Bear was in a bad mood.
As he wandered through the snowy woods,
his grumbling sounded like distant thunder,
scaring all the other animals into hiding.
He was not a happy bear at all.
Bear did not know that it was best to take
a long nap during the wild winds of winter.

"I hate this snow!" he moaned as he froze.
"It's now so cold it hurts my toes!"
Bear was brilliant at complaining.

He came to the edge of a large frozen lake.
It was a huge glittering plate of ice.
Blinded by the reflection, Bear tripped over
something small and green, and fell flat
on his face in the freezing snow.

"Ow, my toes!" Bear howled, furious.
Looking to see what had tripped him,
he saw a small green turtle.

"What are you doing in my way,
Slowcoach-on-legs?"

"Who...are...you...calling...slow?"
replied Turtle, in a long drawn-out drawl.

"Well, I don't see anyone else here,
Mister-Nought-to-Sixty-in-Five-Years!"
said Bear, very rudely.

"How dare you insult a turtle!
We may look slow, but we can move
surprisingly fast!" Turtle sniffed,
getting quite upset.

"Move fast? Huh! I could beat you
in any race, hands down,
easy peasy pudding and pie!"
yawned Bear.

This was too much for Turtle.
Thoughts and ideas raced round his head.
Quick as quick, he announced:
"Okay then, Mr Speedy, let's have a race
to see who really is the fastest of them all!"

"Mighty fine by me!" said Bear, "It'll be a walkover.
You might as well give up now, oh Slithery-Sloth!
But anyhow, where shall we race?"

"Why!" beamed Turtle, "Along the lake, of course!"
"But how?" asked Bear, whose brain
was as small as his body was big.
"The lake is frozen solid!"

"Well now," Turtle said, scratching
his head as if he were thinking.
"You can run along the bank,
and I will swim along the edge.
I will make holes in the ice and pop
my head out of every one,
until we both reach the end!"
Turtle drew a plan in the snow.
"And we shall meet again
at sunrise tomorrow to see
who is the fastest –
Bear or Turtle!"

"Wonderful!" answered Bear.
"Yet another chance to prove that I am
the quickest, slickest, fly-by-fur in town!"
And Bear ambled off, smiling to himself.

Now, do you think that Turtle was worried?
For how can a tiny turtle take on a big, bold bear?
It's impossible! Surely it cannot be done! Or can it...?

The very next day, the sun rose
and painted the sky
like a chieftain's head-dress.
Bear arrived bright and early,
and did fifty star jumps
and one hundred press ups
by the side of the lake.
That was just for starters!

"Are you ready, Turtle?" he hollered.
Bear was now full of beans and raring to go.

He peered over the lake and noticed
a neat row of holes punched in the ice
in a straight line, heading across the lake.
Turtle suddenly popped his head out
of the first hole.

"Good morning, Bear. I'm as ready
as only a clever turtle can be!"

Bear had no idea what Turtle meant.
But now, it was time to get serious.
He knelt down at the starting point.
"On your marks, get set, GO!"

Bear was off like lightning! Each step shook the trees
as he thundered past. Why, even Great Eagle
would be jealous of his turn of speed!

Turtle's head vanished from the first hole.
But before Bear could even blink his eye,
Turtle's head popped up out of the second hole!

"Luck!" growled Bear and he charged on, challenging even the wind, as he whistled through the woods.

But before Bear could take another breath,
Turtle's head popped out of the third hole!

"A fluke!" howled Bear, who was *bearly* ahead by now.
His legs went into overdrive, leaping like lions
through a desert of snow.

But before he could even work out how,
or understand why, Turtle's head popped out
of the fourth hole! Turtle's head was now *ahead!*

Bear sagged! Bear slowed!
His breath struggled out in little steaming puffs,
as he floundered and blundered towards the finish.

Quick as the click of a finger,
Turtle's head popped up out of holes number...

Five...

Six...

Seven...

Eight...

... and finally, hole number Nine!
Turtle's head bowed slowly, as he waited for Bear.
"The race, I think, is mine!"

Bedraggled Bear dragged his bulk to the finish line.
He lay sobbing in a heavy heap, beating his chest
and wailing, "I failed!" Slowly, quietly, he got to his paws
and walked away without another word.

As soon as Bear was out of sight,
Turtle tapped the ice with his claw.
Immediately, eight other turtles popped
their heads up through the holes in the ice!
They were Turtle's brothers and sisters,
who all looked alike!

Together they all cheered.

Once bold, now beaten, Bear slunk away.
He was so tired, he crept into a cave
and slept the rest of the cold season through,
as he does every winter to this day.

"Well done to the Turtle family!
It simply goes to show
that our brains are really the quickest,
though our bodies might be slow!"